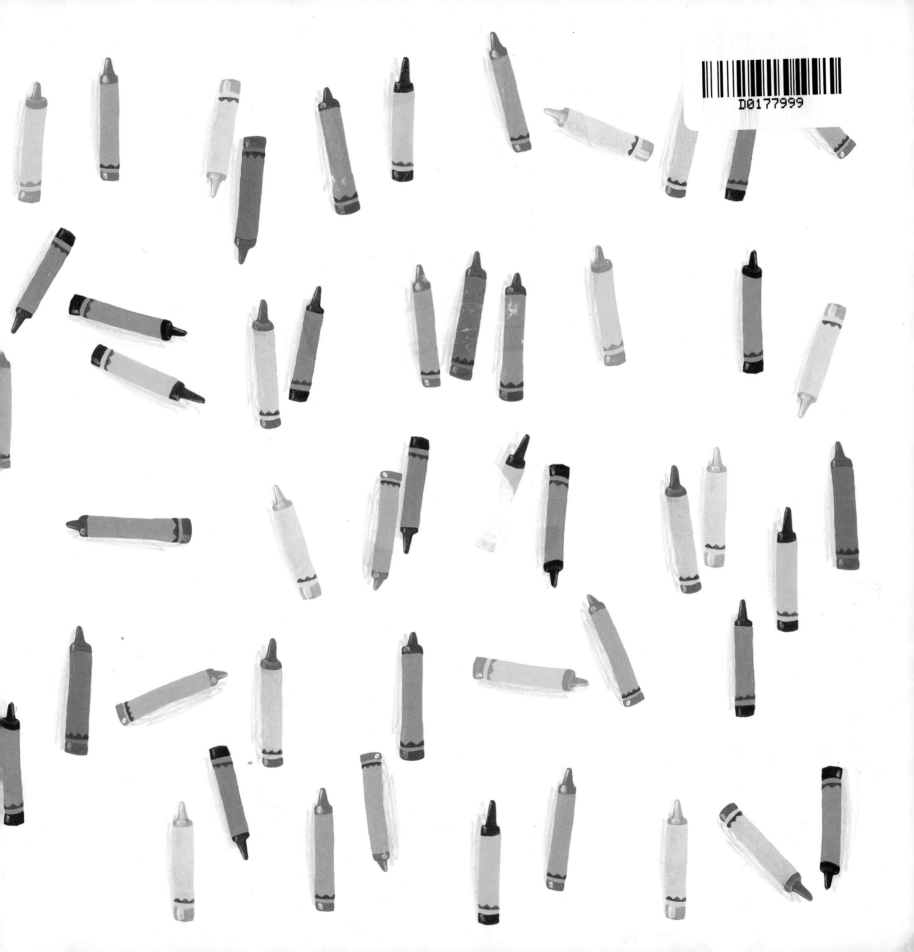

To Marichelle, Abigail and Reese —D.D.

To Ewan —O.J.

THE DAY the CRAYONS QUIT

12 IN A BOX

CRAYONS

WE'RE NOT HAPPY

By DREW DAYWALT

PICTURES by OLIVER JEFFERS

HarperCollins *Children's Books*

One day in class, Duncan went
to take out his crayons and found
a stack of letters with his name
on them.

Hey DUNCAN,

It's me, RED Crayon. WE NEED to talk.
You make me work harder than
any of your other crayons.
All year long I wear myself out
colouring FIRE ENGINES, APPles,
strawberries and EVERYTHING
ELSE that's RED.
I even work on Holidays!
I have to colour all the SANTas
at CHRISTMAS and ALL the
HEArts on VAlentine's day!
I NEED A REST!

Your overworked friend,
RED Crayon

Dear Duncan,

All right, LISTEN.

I love that I'm your favourite crayon for grapes, dragons and wizards' hats, but it makes me crazy that so much of my gorgeous colour goes outside the lines. If you DON'T START COLOURING INSIDE the lines soon... I'm going to COMPLETELY LOSE IT.

Your very neat friend,

Purple Crayon

Dear Duncan,

I'm tired of being called
"light brown" or "Dark tan"
because I am neither.
I am BEIGE and I am proud.
I'm also tired of being second
place to Mr Brown Crayon.
It's not fair that Brown gets
all the bears, ponies and puppies
while the only things I get
are turkey dinners (if I'm lucky)
and wheat, and let's be honest -
when was the last time you
saw a kid excited about
colouring wheat?

Your BEIGE Friend,
Beige Crayon

Duncan,

GREY CRAYON here. You're KILLING ME!
I know you love Elephants. And I
know that elephants are grey...
but that's a LOT of space to colour
in all by myself.
And don't even get me started on
your rhinos, hippos and
HUMPBACK WHALES...
you know how tired I am after
handling one of those things?
such BIG animals...
Baby penguins are grey, you know.
So are very tiny rocks. Pebbles. How about
one of those once in a while to give
me a break?

Your very tired friend,
GREY Crayon

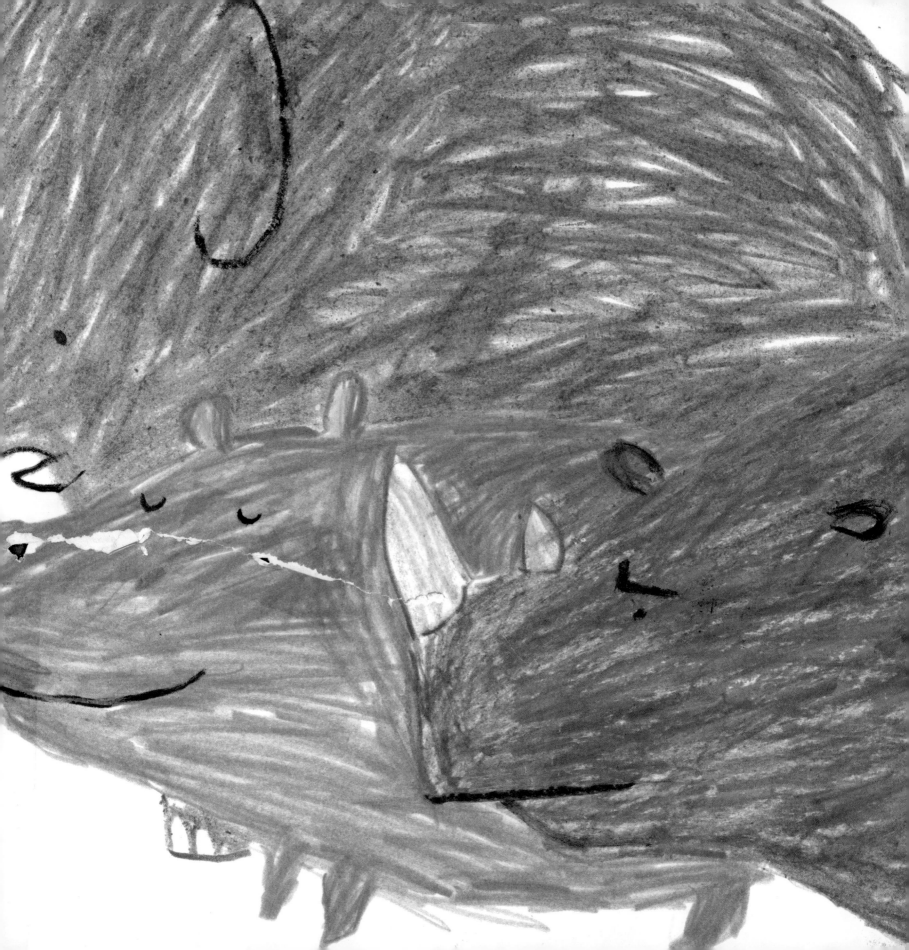

Dear Duncan,
You colour with me, but why? most of the time I'm the same colour as the page you are using me on – WHITE.
If I didn't have a black outline, you wouldn't even know I was THERE!
I'm not even in the rainbow. I'm only used to colour SNOW or to fill in empty space between other things. And it leaves me feeling... ...well... empty. We need to talk.
Your empty friend,
white crayon

white cat
in the snow
by
Duncan

Hi, Duncan,

I HATE being used to draw ~~the~~ the outline of things...

...things that are coloured in by other colours, all of which think they're brighter than me! It's NOT FAIR when you use me to draw a nice beach ball and then fill in the colours of the ball with ALL THE OTHER CRAYONS. How about a BLACK Beach ball some time? Is that too much to ask?

Your friend,
Black Crayon

Dear Duncan,

As Green crayon, I am writing for two reasons. One is to say that I like my work-loads of crocodiles, trees, dinosaurs and frogs. I have no problems and wish to congratulate you on a very successful "colouring things GREEN" career so far.

The second reason I write is for my friends, Yellow crayon and Orange crayon, who are no longer speaking to each other. Both crayons feel THEY should be the colour of the sun.

Please settle this soon because they're driving the rest of us CRAZY!

Your happy friend, Green Crayon

Dear Duncan,

Yellow crayon here. I need you to tell orange crayon that I am the colour of the sun. I would tell him but we are no longer speaking. And I can PROVE I'm the colour of the SUN too! Last Tuesday, you used me to colour in the sun in your "HAPPY FARM" colouring book. In case you're forgotten, it's on page 7. You CAN'T MISS me. I'm shining down brilliantly on a field of YELLOW CORN!

Your pal (and the true colour of the sun),

Yellow crayon

Happy Farm

Dear Duncan,

I see Yellow crayon already talked to you, the BIG WHINER. Anyway, could you please tell Mr Tattletale that he IS NOT the colour of the sun? I would, but we're no longer speaking. We both know I am clearly the colour of the SUN because, on Thursday you used me to colour the sun on BOTH the "Monkey Island" and the "meet the zookeeper" pages in your "DAY AT THE ZOO" colouring book. Orange you glad I'm here? Ha!

Your Pal (and the real colour
                              of the sun),

Orange Crayon

Meet the Zookeeper

Monkey Island

Dear DUNCAN,

It has been great being your FAVOURITE colour this PAST year. And the year before. And the YEAR before ~~that~~ THAT!

I have really enjoyed all those OCEANS, Lakes, Rivers, raindrops, rain CLOUDS and CLEAR skies.

But the BAD NEWS is that I am so short and stubby, I can't even see over the railing in the CRAYON BOX anymore!

I need a BREAK!

Your very stubby friend,
Blue Crayon

Duncan,

Okay, LISTEN HERE, KID!
You have not used me ONCE in ~~the~~
the past year.
It's because you think I am a GIRLS'
colour, isn't it? Speaking of which,
please tell your little sister I
said thank you for using me to colour
in her "Pretty PRINCess" colouring
book. I think she did a fabulous
job of staying inside the lines!
    Now, back to us. Could you PLEASE
use me sometime to colour the occasional
PINK DINOSAUR or MONSTER or
COWBoy? Goodness knows they could
use a splash of colour.
Your unused friend,
Pink crayon

HEY DUNCAN,

It's me, PEACH CRAYON.

WHY did you peel off my paper wrapping??

Now I'm NAKED and too embarrassed to leave the crayon box.

I don't even have ~~a~~ any underwear! How would YOU like to go to school naked? I need some clothes. HELP!

Your naked friend,

PEACH crayon

DUNCAN

Dear Dun...
yellow cra...
to tell ...
the colour o...
...him but we...
I can PRO...
...sun too!
...me to...
"HAPP...

'cuhs"
...Crayon
orange: ...glad...
colour...
he...
...DAY at the...
the Zookeeper,
"Monkey..."
because, a...
...king island...
...colour on the...
...plaid, but

Both cra...
be the c...
Please ...
they're CRA-...
Your

Duncan

book. I...
job of s...
Now, back...
use me some...
PINK DINOSAU...
Cowboy? Goodness...
use a splash of colour.
your unused friend,
Pink crayon

Hi,
O,
I
H
...
but
th...

...your the occasional
MONSTER ...knows they could
...GIRLS'
...which, I
...colour

...te crayon
...ts' splash hats
Your BEIGE fri...
Beige crayon

Well, poor Duncan just wanted to colour . . .
and of course he wanted his crayons to
be happy. And that gave him an idea.

When Duncan showed his teacher his new picture,
she gave him a "good work" sticker for colouring . . .

. . . and a gold star for creativity!

First published in hardback in the USA by Philomel Books, an imprint of Penguin Young Readers Group, in 2013
First published in hardback in Great Britain by HarperCollins Children's Books in 2013

3 5 7 9 10 8 6 4 2

ISBN: 978-0-00-751375-8

HarperCollins Children's Books is a division of HarperCollins Publishers Ltd.

Text copyright © Drew Daywalt 2013
Illustrations copyright © Oliver Jeffers 2013

The art for this book was made with ...um ... crayons. And with the help of a few little friends –
Frieda, Leni, Mia, Shay, Peadar, Logan and particularly Ewan.

Visit our website at: www.harpercollins.co.uk

Printed in China

Significant
Author